COLONIAL PEOPLE

The Colonial Slave Family

LAURA L. SULLIVAN

Cavendish Square
New York

Published in 2016 by Cavendish Square Publishing, LLC
243 5th Avenue, Suite 136, New York, NY 10016

First Edition

Website: cavendishsq.com

CPSIA Compliance Information: Batch #WS15CSQ

Library of Congress Cataloging-in-Publication Data

Sullivan, Laura L., 1974-
The colonial slave family / Laura L. Sullivan.
pages cm. — (Colonial people)
Includes bibliographical references and index.
ISBN 978-1-50260-486-6 (library bound) ISBN 978-1-50260-487-3 (ebook)
1. Slavery—United States—History—18th century—Juvenile literature. 2. African Americans—History—18th century—Juvenile literature.
3. United States—History—Colonial period, ca. 1600-1775—Juvenile literature. I. Title.

E441.S9745 2015
306.3'62097309033—dc23

2015001331

Editorial Director: David McNamara
Editor: Andrew Coddington
Copy Editor: Cynthia Roby
Art Director: Jeffrey Talbot
Designer: Stephanie Flecha
Senior Production Manager: Jennifer Ryder-Talbot
Production Editor: Renni Johnson
Photo Research: J8 Media

The photographs in this book are used by permission and through the courtesy of: North Wind Picture Archives, cover; MPI/Getty Images, 4; Valley of the Nobles, Thebes, Egypt/Bridgeman Images, 7; Jun/File:Roman collared slaves - Ashmolean Museum.jpg/Wikimedia Commons, 8; Public domain/File:Reeve and Serfs.jpg/Wikimedia Commons, 11; Everett Historical/Shutterstock.com, 15, 17; Universal History Archive/UIG/Getty images, 20; Public domain/File:WhippedGordonHarpers.jpg/Wikimedia Commons, 21; The Colonial Williamsburg Foundation, 23; Public domain/File:Slaves working in the tobacco sheds on a plantation (1670 painting).jpg/Wikimedia Commons, 25; Public domain/Library of Congress/File:Phillis Wheatley frontispiece.jpg/Wikimedia Commons, 26; Private Collection/Look and Learn/Bridgeman Images, 30; The Colonial Williamsburg Foundation, 31; North Wind Picture Archives, 32; The Colonial Williamsburg Foundation, 34; MPI/Getty Images, 36; Kenneth C. Zirkel/E+/Getty Images, 41.

Printed in the United States of America

CONTENTS

ONE

The History of Slavery

The practice of **slavery** has been in existence since the earliest recorded history. Though not every ancient culture had slaves, it was common among many groups to keep people as property. There are variations of slavery, but all versions consider certain human beings to be property, without individual rights. In some cultures and at some times, slaves were more or less equal with servants, might live very closely with their **masters**, earn money, and even own slaves themselves. In other situations, a slave was considered an expendable piece of human machinery that could be worked to death or killed by his master.

Slavery was a common practice in most regions of colonial America. Most of the Founding Fathers owned slaves, including George Washington, pictured here on his hourse at his Mount Vernon estate.

Becoming a Slave

People could become slaves in a variety of ways. The most common was probably to be captured during war. After a battle, any captured fighters, as well as women and children living in the defeated villages, could be taken as prizes of war and turned into slaves. People who committed a crime might also be sentenced to slavery.

Sometimes people became slaves for financial reasons. Someone unable to pay off a **debt** might be made a slave. A person without any work prospects might also sell themselves into slavery to an upper-class household, hoping for a better life. Orphan children could become slaves, and some parents unable to care for a large family might sell some of their children into slavery. In many cultures, the child of a slave was considered to be a slave, too.

Ancient Slavery

The very first cultures, made up of hunter-gatherer tribes, probably did not have slavery, or it was not widespread. Most historians believe that the practice of slavery grew with the rise of agriculture. People were living in larger groups, more land and labor were needed to feed them, and conflict and conquest became more common.

When big, city-based civilizations such as those in ancient Egypt began to develop, people needed a large source of cheap labor to provide food. They often used slaves.

Greece and Rome

The English who colonized the Americas were very influenced by ancient Greek and Roman culture, as well as by biblical laws and morality. All of these societies permitted slavery.

The majority of ancient Greeks owned at least one slave. They might work in a private home as servants, or they might be part of a large laboring force working on a farm or in a mine or quarry. Most Greek slaves were captured during war or piracy. A slave might be freed by his master, or he might save enough money to buy his own freedom.

Romans had even more slaves than Greeks. As their empire expanded, they took slaves from Britain, Gaul (present-day France), Germany, Greece, and from many regions in the Middle East. Greek

Many ancient Romans owned slaves such as those depicted here bound together with a slave collar.

slaves were considered to be among the most valuable, because they were thought to be clever and cultured. Romans often used Greek slaves to tutor their children.

Many Roman slaves were highly educated—they might be teachers or doctors. They could earn their own money, own property (though it was actually considered to belong to their master by extension), and could buy their freedom. Gladiators were generally slaves, though a few were volunteers. Other slaves had brief, miserable lives in mines or mills. A slave could be beaten or killed without trial, and his testimony wasn't admitted in court unless it was given under torture.

Biblical Slavery

The Judeo-Christian Bible makes reference to slavery, and was often used to justify the practice. Male Israelite slaves would be freed every seventh year, but female and non-Israelite slaves might be enslaved for life. Family, servants, and slaves were all considered to belong to the **patriarchal** household, under the mastery of the eldest male in the family. Often all levels of the family, including servants and slaves, lived and worked together. According to the New Testament, slaves must obey their masters, but masters should treat slaves well—even as brothers.

The Middle Ages

By about 1000 CE, slaves had been replaced by **serfs** in much of Europe. A serf is a kind of peasant who is bonded not to a master but to the land. The serf was required to work the lord's land, and in return the lord would allow him to grow some food for himself, and would also protect him. A master could not sell his serfs, but he could sell the land to which they were attached. The serfs would then have to work the same land under a new lord. Slavery remained common in the British Isles throughout the Middle Ages.

When Vikings raided along the British and European coasts, they captured people for the slave trade. Some they kept as **thralls**. Most, however, were sold to Islamic countries, which had an active slave trade. North African Barbary pirates continued to capture Europeans through the early nineteenth century. Some were ransomed back to their families, but many were kept as slaves.

Slavery in England

By the time colonists settled in North America, there was little official slavery in England. England did have the workhouse, a kind of forced servitude similar to slavery in which a poor person—including orphans and the very elderly—would be forced to labor.

In the middle ages, slavery was mostly replaced by serfdom, but slavery persisted in England.

They received food, housing, and medicine, but had no choice but to work.

England also had **indentured servants**, who might be criminals or debtors that would be sent to a colony and forced to labor as virtual slaves for a fixed period. An indentured servant could be bought and sold, or beaten, but still had some rights. In most cases, they were eventually freed. Some even sold themselves into indentured servitude in exchange for passage to the New World and the chance at a new life.

There were black people in England in the seventeenth and eighteenth centuries, but their status is unclear. The laws did not specify whether any person in England could be a slave. Still, in the mid-1700s, there were as many as ten thousand black people living in London. Some were free, and some were considered slaves.

Slavery in the Colonies

Though slavery wasn't widely practiced in the homeland, Britain was extremely active in the Atlantic slave trade. Slavery was allowed in all of the thirteen colonies, and persisted in America through the Revolutionary War (1775–1783) up until the American Civil War (1861–1865).

Most black people in the first years of the Jamestown Colony were treated as indentured servants. Many eventually became free. Some later owned property, and a few later owned slaves themselves. Gradually, though, the laws began to change. Laws were passed making black people in the colonies slaves for life (though they could be freed by their masters).

Black children were also condemned to slavery. Though it was the usual British and colonial practice that all inheritance of titles and status was through the father's line, the colonies decided that the state of slavery was inherited through the maternal line. If a person's mother was a slave, he was a slave for life.

TWO

The Slave Trade

Slavery had been an institution in the New World since the first Europeans arrived. The earliest Spanish explorers enslaved the majority of the local population and put them to work—first in mines digging for gold and silver, and later on **plantations**. Vast numbers of the Native people died from harsh treatment and from diseases brought by Europeans. Later, they imported African slaves to take their place.

The Spanish Idea of Slavery

The Spanish and Portuguese had a different attitude toward black slaves than the English colonists later did. Spain and Portugal are both close to Africa, and they had had centuries of contact with Africans. Though the black slaves were property, they could be freed. Once free, no stigma was automatically attached to them based on the color of their skin. In Latin America, slaves often had rights. They could own property, marry, and petition a court to set the price of their freedom. Children of European and African parents generally had the same rights as other free people.

To the Spanish and Portuguese, slavery was a state that could be overcome. Under English colonial law, slavery was a more or less permanent state defined by the color of a person's skin. Even if a slave had been freed, that person would be forever known as a former slave. For Spanish and Portuguese, slavery was only a status. English colonists saw it as a matter of **race**.

A Need for Labor

The settlers in the thirteen colonies desperately needed workers. Particularly in the Southern colonies where agriculture dominated, people were needed to labor on tobacco, indigo, cotton, sugar cane, and rice plantations. At first they tried to fill this labor shortage with indentured servants—white British citizens who were bound to work for a set period of years. But it proved hard to lure enough volunteers for these harsh working conditions, and the colonists turned to African slave labor.

Slaves were crowded onto ships for the terrible Middle Passage from Africa to the Americas. Many died during the crossing.

The first slaves in the colonies were brought from the Caribbean islands. Later, most slaves brought to the colonies were imported directly from Africa.

Slavery in Africa

Slavery had existed in Africa long before Europeans began purchasing slaves there. Though slaves were taken from many parts of Africa, most of the slave trade took place in western Africa. There was variation among the cultures in that region, but most were divided in kingdoms, with hereditary rulers at the top of the social scale. Agricultural workers, or peasants, were at the bottom of society, and below even them came the slaves.

Wars between kingdoms were common, and most slaves were prisoners of war. They might also be criminals or debtors, or people sold into slavery by their families. They usually lived as part of the household and could be disciplined by the head of the household—as could other family members. But they still had many rights. They could testify in court, hold property, and buy their freedom. A female slave who married a free man became free herself.

When Europeans sought African slaves, they usually did not capture slaves themselves. Rather, they made deals with the local kings to purchase slaves.

The Triangular Trade

English, Dutch, Portuguese, and French slavers participated in the slave trade. Dealing in slaves became part of what is known as the **triangular trade**. Slaves were purchased in Africa and sent to the Americas, where they were used to produce agricultural products such as sugar, cotton, and tobacco. These raw materials were then sent to England and the rest of Europe, where they were sold. Sugar might be made into rum, and raw cotton into finished cloth or clothes. Britain and other European countries sent these manufactured goods as well as weapons and tools to Africa to be sold in return for more slaves. The cycle continued.

Purchasing a Slave

Some African kings waged war on neighboring tribes solely to capture slaves to sell. When a village was attacked by a group with guns, everyone who lived there might be captured. They were then shackled together in a line called a **coffle**. Near the coast, they would be transferred to a slave fort where they awaited being purchased.

Slaves in both Africa and in the colonies were often transported chained together in lines called coffles.

When a buyer's ship sailed into a harbor, the slaves would be herded into a courtyard and inspected by a ship's surgeon or captain. Anyone who was sick, over thirty-five, gray-haired, or toothless was set aside. Those who weren't sold would usually be killed to spare the expense of feeding them. Those who were young and healthy would be bought and soon loaded onto the slave ship.

In all, some eighteen million people were removed from Africa and sold as slaves. Up to 2.4 million Africans died on the journey

Rebellion on a Slave Ship

Many slaves rebelled against being held in bondage, both on the ship and later. Some fought while at sea, but this was difficult. Even if they overpowered the crew, it was unlikely that the slaves would have known how to pilot the ship to safety.

More common forms of rebellion were refusing to eat and **suicide**. Slaves who didn't eat might be tortured or force-fed. The most common form of suicide was jumping overboard. The belief was that that they would be reunited with their families and friends in the afterlife. Members of the Kru ethnic group (present-day Liberia and Sierra Leone) fought so hard and committed suicide so often that slavers eventually stopped trading them.

across the Atlantic, which was known as the **Middle Passage**, and more died after arrival in the Americas.

The Middle Passage

It was said that a person could smell a slave ship from miles away. The captured men, women, and children were generally naked, often chained, and usually confined to small areas in the airless hold of the ship. A man was given a space measuring 72 by 18 inches (183 by 46 centimeters). A woman was allowed 70 by 16 inches (178 by 41 cm). It was said they had less room than a corpse lying in a coffin. A few buckets were the only bathrooms, and they usually overflowed. Many became seasick, or ill from diarrhea.

After the ship had been at sea for several days the slaves might sometimes be brought to the deck. There they might be washed with seawater, or forced to dance to "dispel **melancholia**." Though the women were sometimes unchained, the men usually stayed chained. They were fed beans, yams, and rice, and a half-pint of water with each meal.

Slaves in the Colonies

Slavers docked at Chesapeake Bay, Charleston, South Carolina, and elsewhere. Only about 5 percent of the slaves taken from Africa were brought to the colonies. Most were taken to the Caribbean and South America.

A purchaser—most often a prosperous farmer or plantation owner, but also wealthy craftsmen and artisans, merchants, or anyone with money—would come and inspect the slaves. The purchase might be made privately, or the slaves might be sold auction-style, going to the highest bidder. The slaves could be sick or malnourished from their long, difficult journey, so the slaver might wash them, dye any gray hairs, and give them alcohol to make them seem healthier.

Any family bonds or friendships the captured Africans might have made on the ship were torn apart when the slaves were sold.

The prospective owner was free to poke, prod, and intimately examine the slaves.

The price of a slave varied. In 1705, a healthy male slave might cost about £30 or more. Later, after the American Revolutionary War (1775–1783) and into the nineteenth century, when there were bans on importing new slaves, the price was much higher.

After they were purchased, the slaves were transported to their new homes. Any family they might have traveled with, any friends they made aboard the ship, were gone forever. Yet a slave might forge new connections, even a family. It all depended on where he was sold.

THREE

Slave Life in the Colonies

There was tremendous variation in the life of a slave in the colonies. They might live almost as a member of their owner's family and be treated with kindness and consideration, educated, or trained in a trade. Conversely, they might be worked almost to death, beaten for the slightest infraction, or even killed by their master without a trial. In either case, a slave had almost no rights and was completely subject to the whims of his or her owner.

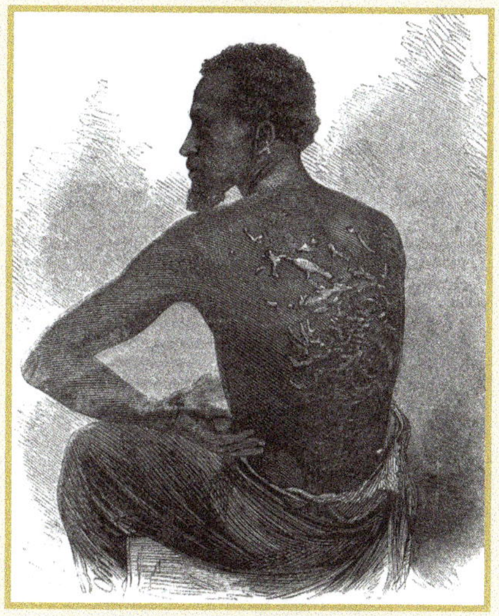

A slave was at the mercy of his master. He or she might be beaten or even killed for any reason, or for no reason at all.

It is difficult to examine the life of a slave family in any region of the colonies, because slaves were not often permitted to have families. They generally associated with other slaves owned by their master.

If they formed unions and had children, their families might be split up at any time if their owner decided to sell them. Still, some slaves did manage to have a family life, and beyond that formed tight-knit community relationships.

A Slave in the Northern Colonies

Most of the northern colonial lands were not suitable for large-scale agriculture, so they did not tend to develop the massive plantation structure of slavery common in the southern colonies. Most northern slaves lived on small farms or in towns.

Though Massachusetts was the first colony to have African slaves, it also gave those slaves considerable rights in the first century of colonization. **Puritans** took a biblical view of slavery—it was a person's right to have slaves, but the master should be a benevolent patriarch and tend to them as he did his family, servants, and all of his dependents. The Puritan ethic of hard work also frowned on the idea of turning all labor over to a slave, so many Puritans worked alongside their slaves.

Slave Laws Change

Early in the seventeenth century blacks in the north, whether enslaved or free, received the protection of law, could testify in

Slaves were condemned to a life of hard work and suffering. Some held so-called privileged positions in the household, caring for children or as companions or assistants. No matter the advantages or disadvantages, none of them were free.

court, and received the same punishments as free white citizens if they committed a crime. Until 1705, black and white people could marry. The children were free, and the fathers were responsible for their care.

Later, slave laws came more in line with those in the southern colonies. Slaves generally did not have the protection of law and could not testify in court. Still, there was always a stronger emancipation movement in the north than in the South. Despite the new laws, Puritans tended to treat their slaves comparatively well. The religious group known as **Quakers** was against slavery, and by the end of the eighteenth century nearly all Quakers had renounced slave ownership.

Marriage and Family

Most slaves were male in the early colonial period. Later, though, women were also brought to the colonies. In northern colonies, where fewer people owned slaves (and those who did generally didn't own many), it was more difficult for a slave to marry and form a family simply because it was hard for them to meet other slaves. Often, slave owners could only afford one or two slaves. In fact, slaves had been sold for no fault other than bearing children. The master might be able to support a few slaves but not a slave family, so the woman and children might be sold, together or separately.

If a slave in a Puritan household got married, however, the bond tended to be lifelong—like that of a free marriage. Puritan-owned slaves were usually married by clergy. Their masters respected the marriage vows. They would not be sold separately, and their children would remain with the household.

A Slave in the Southern Colonies

The middle and southern colonies were more suited to large-scale agriculture. Huge plantations produced cotton, tobacco, and rice.

Many slaves in the South worked on plantations, such as these slaves working in the sheds of a tobacco plantation.

Wealthy landowners would have dozens or hundreds of slaves to perform the arduous work of cultivation and harvest. Though laws offered slaves little or no protection, the early colonial system of slavery tended to be slightly better than slavery after the American Revolution.

The Task System

Nineteenth-century plantations during the Civil War used the gang system of slavery. This means that teams of slaves performed a task—picking cotton, for example—for a set number of hours every day under an overseer. They did the same job all day, and could not stop except for a brief meal. During the colonial period the task system was used. This system was particularly common in the rice-growing region of the Carolinas and Georgia.

Under the task system, each slave was given a certain job to do for the day. For example, he or she would be told to dig a certain length of canal or plant a certain number of rows of rice. When the

Phillis Wheatley, Slave Poet

Phillis Wheatley (1753–1784) was born in West Africa and sold into slavery at age seven. She was sold to the progressive Wheatley family of Boston. They taught her to read and write English, Latin, and Greek. Few females of any race received such an education. When Phillis began writing poetry, the Wheatleys encouraged her. In 1773 her collection *Poems on Various Subjects, Religious and Moral*, was published in England and later in the colonies. George Washington met her and praised her work.

Phillis was freed when her master died, but fell into hard times. She married a free black grocer, but their two young children died, and they struggled financially. Her husband was eventually sent to prison for debt. Though Phillis published a few more poems, she found no more real success. She was forced to work as a scullery maid. Soon afterward, she and her infant child died from an illness.

Phillis Wheatley received an exceptional education and became a published poet.

job was complete, they would be able to live their own lives. The work was hard and dangerous—most of it took place in swamps filled with alligators, snakes, and mosquitoes. Still, the system gave the slaves a certain amount of **autonomy**. At the end of the day, slaves could tend their own gardens, hunt or fish, work for another farm for money, or gather for social activities.

Family Life on a Plantation

Whether under the task or gang system, slaves on a large farm or plantation tended to have living quarters arranged like a village. Individuals or families would have small, one-room wooden houses, usually without windows or floors, but with a hearth for heat and cooking. They were given an allotment of corn or rice, as well as yams, salted meat, and molasses. In addition to this they had small plots of land on which to grow vegetables. They sometimes raised chickens, rabbits, or pigs for their own use.

Because the slaves lived in a large community, bonds were common—yet most relationships weren't sanctioned by marriage. Instead, couples declared their love in an unofficial ceremony. Some masters encouraged unions, thinking it made the slaves more content and less likely to rebel. Children born to slaves were the property of their master, so families were often encouraged to add to the master's wealth. Some women and couples took measures to avoid having children so there wouldn't be another generation condemned to slavery.

Children

Mothers were the primary leaders of slave families. A mother often had to care for her newborn baby while working. After a while, older children would care for the child. Sometimes there was a special house for children. There, one or several elderly slave women looked them after communally. This provided some security in their lives in case their mothers were sold.

Child mortality was very high. Many slave children died from infections, diarrhea, or poor nutrition. Those who survived were put to work early. A child as young as five or six might be assigned simple tasks, such carrying messages. By the time they were ten or twelve, they would be expected to perform most adult work.

FOUR

The Slave Community

In their homeland in Africa, people were almost always members of a community and family. Family was important, and extended kinship ties were recognized. People knew their place in society and were defined by those to whom they were related. Ancestors were honored, and children to come were anticipated. When these people were enslaved, all that was stripped away. They went from being members of a community to solitary individuals adrift in a harsh new world.

When possible, slaves tried to establish new communities and new family ties when they were sold to the colonies. There were many obstacles. Slaves had no say in where they lived, so any connections made could be broken at any moment.

In their home villages, Africans had close family and social connections, with many generations living together or nearby.

The Slave in the City

Slaves in cities were usually household servants and might spend the majority of their lives inside the house. They would have little opportunity to socialize with any other slaves who did not live with them. It was almost impossible for them to form family ties unless it was with another slave purchased by their master, or if they were freed.

Still, they had the occasional opportunity to make connections with other slaves. Female domestic slaves were often sent on errands to the market. There, they would meet other slaves and exchange news. They might only have a few minutes each week, but it enabled them to form a network of communication. Likewise male slaves in the city, who were often coachmen, would have the chance to meet other slaves when they traveled with their masters to other houses.

A Northern house slave, such as this footman, might have some advantages over his plantation counterparts. However, he probably never had a day off and rarely got to make social connections with other slaves.

The Rural Slave

In rural areas where more slaves lived, there tended to be more connections of kinship and friendship. When a slave lived on a smaller farm, he might travel (with or without permission) to another nearby farm to visit friends. Husbands and wives might even live on different farms, and be allowed to visit each other. Many slaves took part in secret nighttime visits to maintain connections with family and friends.

When slaves had occasional free time they often used it to socialize and to cement bonds of family and friendship. Singing and dancing were common pastimes.

On large farms, it was much easier for slaves to gather and socialize. They generally lived in a village of huts and small houses, and sometimes practiced communal farming or cooking for their own needs. There was much more opportunity to establish friendship and other ties in these large communities.

Religion and Community

Depending on the region, some slave codes forbade slaves to travel in groups or to gather in large groups. The one exception was for religious celebrations. Most Southern plantation slaves had Sunday either entirely or partially off and there was sometimes a four-day holiday at Christmas. Religious meetings became one of the few times slaves could congregate, and the church became important in many slave communities.

The earliest slaves maintained many of the religious practices of their homeland. Many of them came from religions with many gods, including a creator or paramount god, along with lesser gods. There was also acknowledgment of a spirit world, and reverence was paid to ancestors. Though slaves might come from different tribes originally, there were enough similarities that they could find common ground in songs, stories, and rituals.

The Church

After 1800, many slaves converted to Christianity, though many kept aspects of their old religions, too. At first, some slave owners didn't want to convert their slaves, fearing that the law would say no Christian could be enslaved. But when later laws ruled that out, many allowed or even encouraged their slaves to convert.

Some slaves found hope, as well as a place to socialize and plan for a better future, in church.

Church meetings became a focal point of the slave community. Slaves would not only worship, they would socialize, find ways to improve their situations, and sometimes plan rebellions or an escape to freedom. Religious meetings could give hope. Biblical stories about suffering and redemption, and about Moses freeing the slaves in Egypt, would inspire slaves to seek their own freedom.

Colonial Slavery by the Numbers

When the American Revolution began in 1775, about 20 percent of the population in the colonies was either black or of African descent. Most were enslaved. In 1790, only about 8 percent of black people in the colonies were free. More than half of all black people in the colonies lived in Maryland and Virginia. In the Chesapeake region, black people made up about 60 percent of the total population.

In the New England colonies overall, slaves made up about 2–3 percent of the population. However, in major cities such as Boston, slaves made up 20–25 percent of the population.

Few people actually owned slaves. Overall, about 1.4 percent of the colonists were slave owners. Even in the South, only around 5 percent of residents owned any slaves. But many of those slaveholders owned large numbers of slaves. In 1750, one-third of slaves in South Carolina lived on a plantation with fifty or more slaves.

AM I NOT A MAN AND A BROTHER?

FIVE

The Legacy of Slavery

The practice of slavery in colonial America caused the disruption of millions of lives. Many died on the voyage, and those who survived the journey were condemned to a life as property, without rights. Though actual conditions varied, every slave from the first to land on colonial soil to the last slave liberated by the American Civil War (1861–1865) lived without freedom.

Except in a few Quaker communities, and among some individuals, slavery was an accepted, unquestioned policy. Slavery had become essential to the colonial economy, and people looked for reasons to maintain it. Unlike the standards of slavery found in other historical periods, colonial slavery, and the slavery practiced after the colonies

The abolition movement began in the North, but it took a war to eliminate slavery from the entire United States.

became the United States of America in 1776, was based on race. Many people used faulty science to conclude that whites were superior to blacks. Some argued that black people were not capable of living in a state of freedom. These false ideas helped support the perpetuation of slavery.

Gradually, though, some people began to doubt the morality of keeping another person as property. Because there were not as many large-scale farms in the northern colonies, they did not have such a great need for slaves. After the United States declared itself independent of Britain, the northern states gradually outlawed slavery. Vermont banned it in 1777. By 1804, slavery had been abolished in all northern states.

Rich Southern landowners, though, had a vested interest in keeping slaves. Although some freed their slaves—an action that raised the proportion of freed former slaves from one percent to ten percent of the total black population in the South between 1790 and 1810—most clung to the idea of slave ownership.

In 1807 both Britain and the United States banned the slave trade. This meant that ships from those nations could not purchase slaves from Africa or elsewhere and sell them. Though no new slaves could legally enter the United States, the population was already high enough that the slave trade within the states could support itself.

The price of slaves rose considerably. People who had a few slaves often sold to the huge slave-owning plantations in the Deep South for a large profit. Despite the law, slave ships still entered New York, New Orleans, and other harbors to illegally sell slaves.

Slavery in the United States didn't come to an end until after the Civil War. In 1863, President Abraham Lincoln issued the Emancipation Proclamation. After the war, nearly four million slaves were freed. Former slaves made up about 12 percent of the total US population.

The former slaves' problems weren't over. As northern soldiers left, many former slaves were taken back into servitude. They were forced to live in conditions that rivaled those of slavery. Laws excluded black people from many civil rights. With few employment opportunities, many were forced to work as **sharecroppers**. This means that the landowner would allow the former slave work on his land in return for a percentage of the yield. This system was abused. The sharecropper was often forced into debt and had to labor without pay to work it off—essentially becoming enslaved again.

The Southern states also passed "black codes" that attempted to control former slaves and their descendants. Among the worst of these laws was a provision that any black person deemed a "vagrant"—a person without a home or job—could be arrested and assigned to forced labor. Almost any black person could be declared a vagrant, for almost any reason. Though black people were given the right to vote in the Fifteenth Amendment passed in 1870, they were mostly kept from voting with poll taxes and discriminatory testing.

Poll taxes required citizens to pay a fee to register to vote. Many poor African Americans could not afford to pay such a tax and were thereby unable to vote. The literacy test was given to blacks while at the polls. The questions were often confusingly worded. Many were intentionally unanswerable. The registrar, who was white, would be the ultimate judge of whether an answer was correct.

Later, the so-called Jim Crow laws enforced racial segregation in the South. Black people were forbidden to use the same public bathrooms, water fountains, and swimming pools as white people. They were forced to sit in the back seats of all public transportation. Even schools were segregated. These laws were not in the north, but segregation existed all the same. Housing and employment opportunities were often severely restricted for black people.

The Civil Rights Movement of the 1960s led to change. Activists including Martin Luther King Jr. protested by using methods of passive resistance such as sit-ins and marches. The Civil Rights Act of 1964 and the Voting Rights Act of 1965 made it the law that all people be treated equally.

Long after slavery, extreme prejudice continued in the South.

However, the legacy of slavery persists even today. Some think that since slaves and their descendants were not allowed to accumulate the wealth of their labor (as other people could), their heirs today tend to be poorer. In 2009, the wealth gap between black and white people was $326,500. Throughout the United States, 11.6 percent of white people are living below the poverty level, compared to 25.8 percent of blacks. Black people also have a higher arrest rate, suffer stricter enforcement of mandatory minimum sentencing, and have longer jail or prison sentences. The incarceration rate of black males is more than six times higher than that of their white male counterparts. Opinions differ on the exact causes of these disparities, but many think it ultimately traces pack to persistent, historical patterns of discrimination that began in colonial times and echo through black populations today.

There have been positive changes, though. President Barack Obama has shown that in many ways the American ideal of equality is alive and well. Affirmative action policies help ensure that all citizens have equal access to housing, education, and employment regardless of race. Still, the struggle for equality continues for many descendants of the slave families of colonial America.

Reparations

Some people have argued that the descendants of slaves should be paid **reparations**—money meant to compensate for their ancestors' suffering, and make amends for the continued harm caused by the legacy of slavery.

In the past, reparations have been paid to Japanese Americans who were forced to live in internment camps during World War II. They were also paid to some Native Americans after their lands were taken. Those in favor of reparations to the descendants of former slaves argue that reparations would fix the economic imbalance that came about because slaves and freedmen were deprived of just wages for their labor. If slaves and former slaves had been properly paid, they say, African Americans today would be in a much better economic position.

Arguments against reparations point out that it is difficult to properly identify the victims and how much they have been harmed. Also, slaveholders accounted for only about 5 percent of the population in the South (about 1.4 percent of the overall American population). Some argue that if all Americans were taxed for reparations, it would unfairly punish people who were not at fault. Others argue that because African nations were complicit in the slave trade, they should be held equally accountable.

Glossary

autonomy Freedom from control; the right of self-governance.

coffle A line of slaves or animals chained together for transport.

debt Money that is owed and unpaid; the state of owing money.

indentured servant A person who is contracted to labor for another person for a fixed period, often without pay, but frequently in exchange for passage to another country.

master A person who is in charge or control of people working under him, especially servants or slaves.

melancholia A mental state of great depression, sadness, and gloom, often with fear and foreboding.

Middle Passage The journey traveled by slaves across the Atlantic Ocean to the Americas.

patriarch The male head of a family or group; the eldest or dominant male in a family.

plantation A large farm that uses resident labor to cultivate such crops as cotton, tobacco, or sugar cane.

Puritan A Protestant group in England and the New England colonies that opposed many customs of the Church of England; also, any person who favors a strict moral code and is opposed to pleasure.

Quaker A member of the Religious Society of Friends who believes in simplicity and uses no scripture or formal ministry.

race A social concept used to divide humans into groups based on origin, ethnicity, appearance, or other considerations.

reparations Money paid to an individual or group, or their descendants, to compensate for wrongs done to them.

serf A worker bound to labor on a landowner's estate.

sharecropper A farmer, usually a former slave, who works on another person's land and is paid with part of the crop.

slavery The state of being the property of another person, deprived of all or some rights.

suicide Taking one's own life intentionally.

thrall A captive, servant, or slave; the state of being completely in the power of another person.

triangular trade The trading system in which raw materials, such as sugar or cotton from the Americas, were sent to Europe. There they were made into manufactured goods and sent to Africa, where they were traded for slaves, who were sent to the Americas to make the raw materials.

Find Out More

BOOKS

McKissack, Patricia C. *Look to the Hills: The Diary of Lozette Moreau, a French Slave Girl.* New York Colony 1763. New York: Scholastic, 2004.

Tarrant-Reid, Linda. *Discovering Black America: From the Age of Exploration to the Twenty-First Century*. New York: Harry N. Abrams, 2012.

Turner, Glennette Tilley. *Fort Mose and the Story of the Man Who Built the First Free Black Settlement in Colonial America*. New York: Harry N. Abrams, 2010.

WEBSITES

The Colonial Williamsburg Foundation

www.history.org

PBS African American World

www.pbskids.org/aaworld

US History

www.ushistory.org/us/6.asp

MUSEUMS

The National Museum of African American History and Culture

nmaahc.si.edu

This branch of the Smithsonian teaches people about the diverse and rich African American experience.

The Slave Relic Historical Museum

slaverelics.org/blog

This museum in Walterboro, South Carolina, is dedicated to preserving the history of slaves from 1750 to the mid-1800s through actual artifacts, documents, photographs, and memorabilia from the period.

Index

Page numbers in **boldface** are illustrations. Entries in **boldface** are glossary terms.

About the Author

Laura L. Sullivan is the author of many fiction and nonfiction books for children, including the fantasy *Under the Green Hill* and the romance *Love by the Morning Star*. She has also co-written the upcoming romantic mystery *Girl About Town,* set in the Golden Age of Hollywood, with famed director and producer Adam Shankman. She is the author of many books for Cavendish Square, including six titles in the Colonial People series.